W9-BMS-628

Marilea McAllister

T. McCloy

T. McCloy

Are We There Yet?

NANCY CRYSTAL

VLADYANA KRYKORKA

North Winds Press

Text copyright © 1991 by Nancy Crystal.
Illustrations copyright © 1991 by Vladyana Krykorka.
All rights reserved.

No part of this publication may be reproduced or stored
in a retrieval system, or transmitted in any form or by
any means, electronic, mechanical, photocopying, recording,
or otherwise, without written permission of the publisher,
North Winds Press, 123 Newkirk Road, Richmond Hill,
Ontario, Canada L4C 3G5.

6 5 4 3 2 1   Printed in Hong Kong   1 2 3 4 5 6/9

Canadian Cataloguing in Publication Data

Crystal, Nancy
    Are we there yet?

Issued also in French under title: Quand est-ce
qu'on arrive?
ISBN 0-590-73646-9

I. Krykorka, Vladyana. II. Title.

PS8555.R96A7 1991   jC813'54   C91-093600-5
PZ7.C78Ar 1991

For Matthew and Julie.
      —N.C.

To my grandfather Hynek Langer
for teaching me to love animals.
      —V.K.

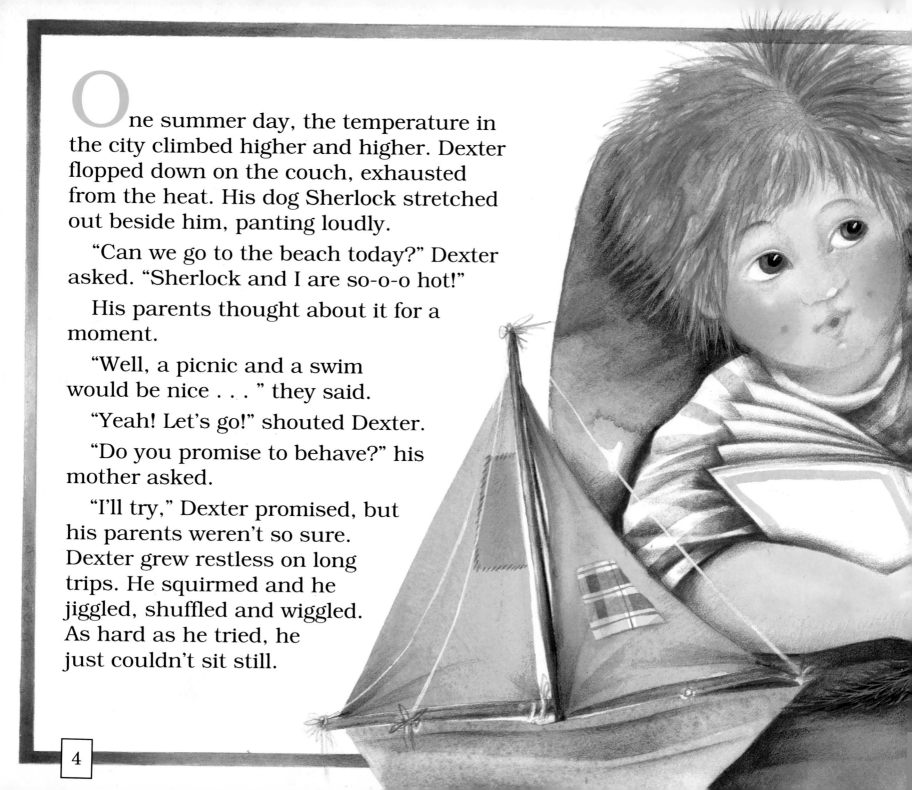

One summer day, the temperature in the city climbed higher and higher. Dexter flopped down on the couch, exhausted from the heat. His dog Sherlock stretched out beside him, panting loudly.

"Can we go to the beach today?" Dexter asked. "Sherlock and I are so-o-o hot!"

His parents thought about it for a moment.

"Well, a picnic and a swim would be nice . . . " they said.

"Yeah! Let's go!" shouted Dexter.

"Do you promise to behave?" his mother asked.

"I'll try," Dexter promised, but his parents weren't so sure. Dexter grew restless on long trips. He squirmed and he jiggled, shuffled and wiggled. As hard as he tried, he just couldn't sit still.

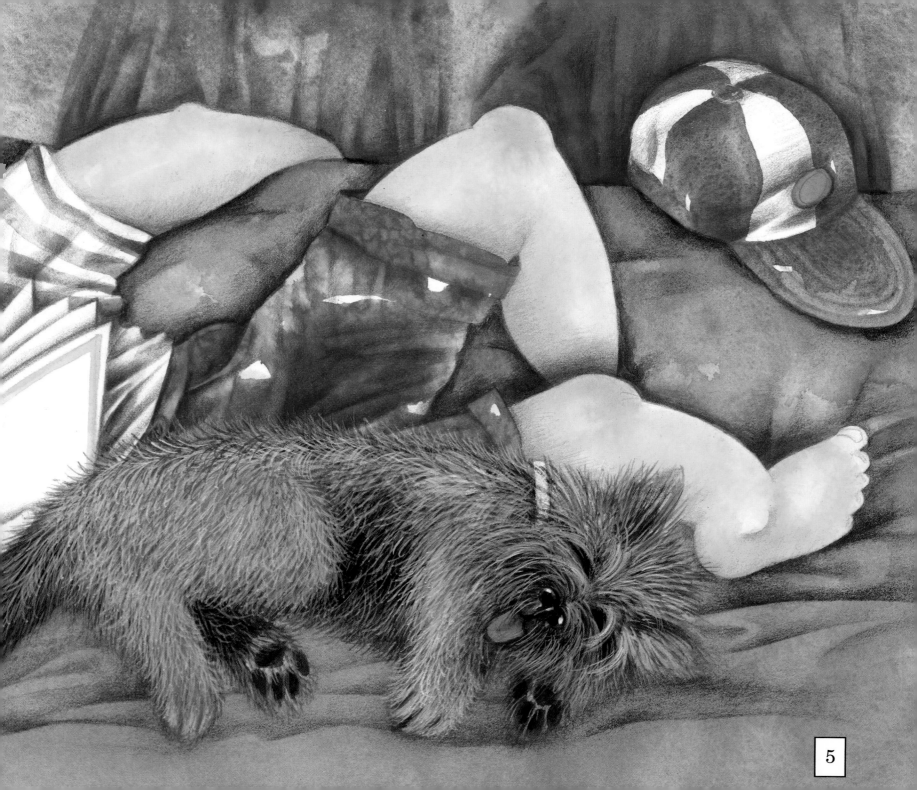

Dexter's parents loaded up the car with all his favourite things: his Walkman and some comic books, a shovel and a pail, his special kite, some bubble gum, a boat with one torn sail, a snorkel and his flippers, a baseball and a mitt, a can of worms, a Frisbee and his brand new fishing kit.

"There, that should keep you busy!" said Mom.

Dexter and Sherlock climbed into the back seat. It was crowded. "Everybody buckled up?" Dad asked.

"Check!" Dexter answered.

Sherlock was not happy. He made low grumbly noises. Dexter's Mom turned around to see what was wrong.

"Dexter," she sighed, "you know Sherlock doesn't wear a seatbelt!"

"But Dad asked if everyone was buckled up!" Dexter replied as he released Sherlock.

"You promised to behave," she reminded him.

"Okay, I'll try," he said.

So off they drove. Past the tall apartment buildings, past the giant skyscrapers reaching for the clouds, past the buses and cars and traffic lights, and onto the highway.

Dexter was getting restless. He squirmed and he jiggled. He shuffled and wiggled.

"Are we there yet?" he asked.

Nobody answered.

uietly, gently, he began drumming on the back of his mother's seat. She tried to ignore it, but soon it felt like she was sitting on a jackhammer. Finally, Mom turned around.

"Dexter, find something to do!" she snapped.

"Okay, I'll try," he replied.

13

Dexter rummaged around the back seat. He picked up his Walkman, and a smile spread across his face. He placed the headphones carefully on Sherlock's head and turned the radio on.

Sherlock began to sing along, wagging his tail to the beat and brushing the top of Dad's head with every swish. The hairs tickled, but Dad tried his best to ignore it.

"Are we there yet?" Dexter asked, making the music a little louder. Sherlock's tail landed on Dad's bald spot like a shaggy wig. Dad couldn't see. He brushed dog hair out of his eyes.

"Dexter, settle down!" Dad said.

"Okay, I'll try," he replied.

Dexter looked out the window
at the rows and rows of corn swaying in the breeze.
Huge bales of hay dotted the fields like a giant
checkerboard. They passed horses and cows lazily
chewing grass in a pasture.

Dexter was restless. He squirmed and he jiggled.
He shuffled and wiggled.

"I'm hungry," he announced.

"We'll have a picnic lunch as soon as we get to
the lake," Mom promised.

Dexter found the package of bubble gum and put two big pieces into his mouth. Soon he was blowing bubbles in Sherlock's face. Sherlock tilted his head to the left and then to the right. He blinked every time one of the bubbles popped.

18

"Watch this, Sherlock," Dexter whispered. He took a deep breath and blew an enormous bubble. The look on Sherlock's face made Dexter laugh. The harder he laughed, the bigger the bubble grew. Sherlock sat up straight and tried to catch the bubble with his paw.

"Are we there yet?" Dexter mumbled. He couldn't talk and blow at the same time.

Dad looked in the mirror to see what was going on.

"Dexter — no! Don't!" Dad begged.

19

It was too late. The bubble popped, all over Dexter and his baseball cap. Sherlock tried to lick it off. Mom spent the next ten minutes picking grape bubble gum out of Sherlock's whiskers.

"Dexter, please settle down!" she sighed.

"Okay, I'll try," Dexter replied.

21

Dexter gazed out the window and tried to read the highway signs and billboards as they whizzed past. Soon he became restless again. He squirmed and he jiggled. He shuffled and wiggled.

"I'm hot," he announced.

His dad took a long, deep breath and counted to ten. His mom bit her lower lip and tapped the map against her hand.

"Why don't you open your window a bit?" she suggested.

23

Dexter rolled down his window.
He kicked off his shoes, tied the laces in
a giant knot and dropped them on the floor.
Kerplunk!

Then he took off his shirt and waved it
out the window, letting it flap in the breeze
like a flag. Suddenly,
a gust of wind sucked
the shirt out of his hand.
Dexter watched in
amazement as it
blew away.

Dexter stared out the window. Then mischief
sparkled in his eyes. Slowly, carefully, he wiggled
out of his pants and held them out the window.

"Are we there yet?" he asked, as his pants
whipped against the side of the car.

"Soon," Mom answered. She turned around just in time to see Dexter's pants sail away.

"Dexter!" she shrieked. "What are you doing?"

"I was hot," he answered.

Mom was furious. "Roll up that window this minute! If you throw one more thing out, we're going right home!"

But Dexter was still hot. He thought for a minute, then took off his socks and put them on Sherlock. Sherlock tilted his head and stared at the socks on his paws. He wanted to scratch but he couldn't with Dexter's socks on.

Dexter sat there wearing nothing but his polka dot shorts.

"Are we there yet?" he asked.

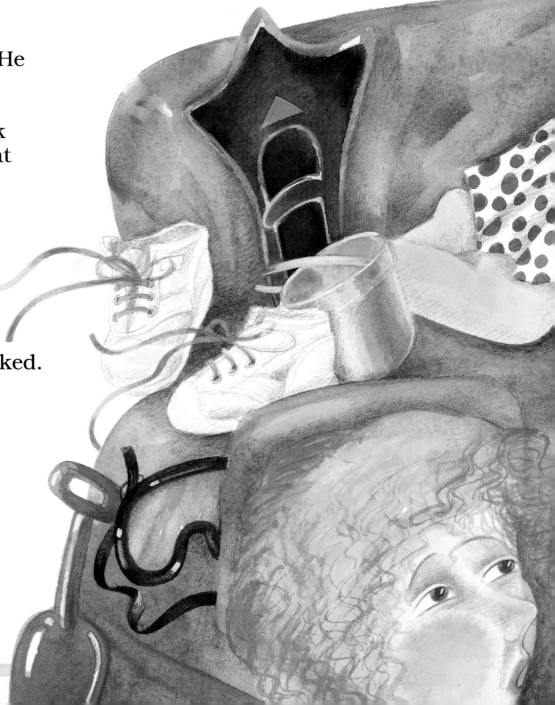

Sherlock began to bark. The entire car shook every time he tried to scratch. Dexter laughed until his sides ached.

Mom rolled her eyes and stared at the ceiling. Dad rubbed his temple and mumbled to himself. They looked at each other and shook their heads.

"Dexter, settle down," they pleaded. "We're nearly there."

"Okay, I'll try," he replied.

29

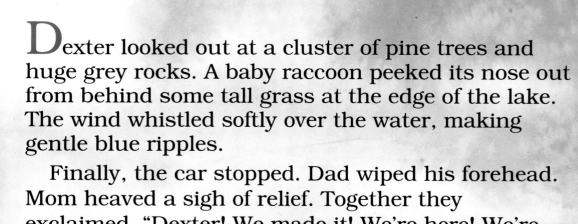

Dexter looked out at a cluster of pine trees and huge grey rocks. A baby raccoon peeked its nose out from behind some tall grass at the edge of the lake. The wind whistled softly over the water, making gentle blue ripples.

Finally, the car stopped. Dad wiped his forehead. Mom heaved a sigh of relief. Together they exclaimed, "Dexter! We made it! We're here! We're finally here!" They turned around and looked in the back seat.

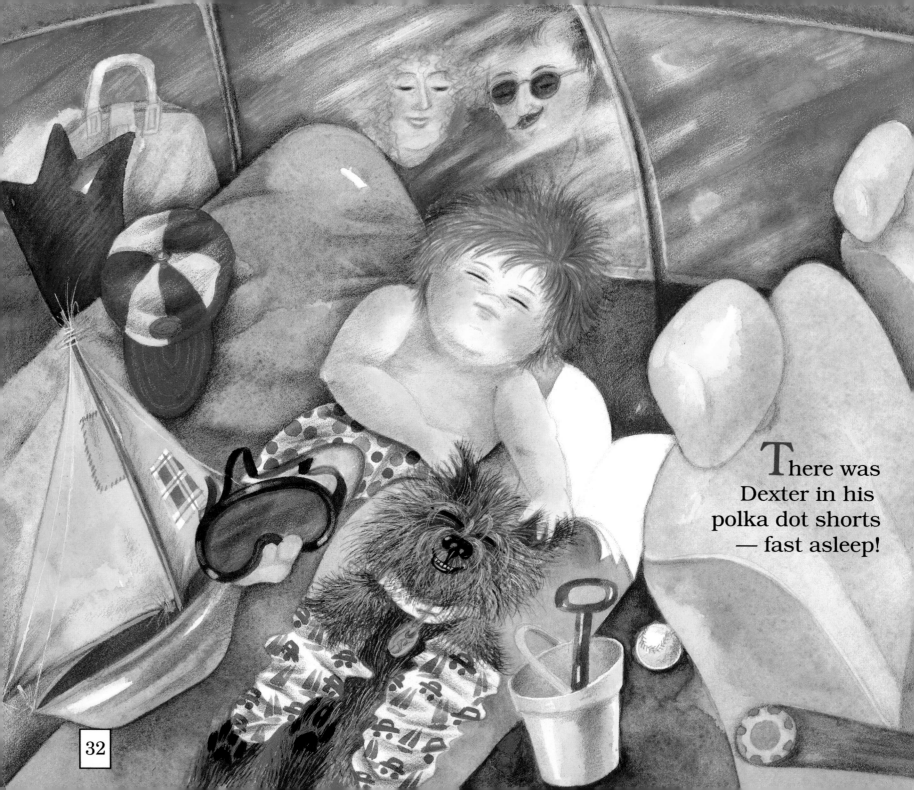

There was Dexter in his polka dot shorts — fast asleep!

Marilea McAllister